About the Author

Francesca Simon is universally known for the staggeringly popular Horrid Henry series. She is also the author of Costa-shortlisted *The Monstrous Child*, which she turned into an opera with composer Gavin Higgins for the Royal Opera House, and two picture books: *Hack and Whack* and *The Goat Café*. She lives in North London with her family.

About the Illustrator

Steve May is an animation director and illustrator. Steve has illustrated books by Jeremy Strong, Philip Reeve, Harry Hill and Phil Earle, as well as the Dennis the Menace series. He lives in North London.

FABER has published children's books since 1929. T. S. Eliot's *Old Possum's Book of Practical Cats* and Ted Hughes' *The Iron Man* were among the first. Our catalogue at the time said that 'it is by reading such books that children learn the difference between the shoddy and the genuine'. We still believe in the power of reading to transform children's lives. All our books are chosen with the express intention of growing a love of reading, a thirst for knowledge and to cultivate empathy. We pride ourselves on responsible editing. Last but not least, we believe in kind and inclusive books in which all children feel represented and important.

TWO TERRIBLE VIKINGS

and **Grunt** the **Berserker**

FRANCESCA SIMON
Illustrated by Steve May

faber

P
PROFILE BOOKS

First published in 2022
by Faber & Faber Limited
Bloomsbury House,
74–77 Great Russell Street,
London WC1B 3DA
faberchildrens.co.uk
and
Profile Books
29 Cloth Fair
London EC1A 7JQ
profilebooks.com

Typeset in Sweater School by MRules
This font has been specially chosen to support reading

Printed by CPI Group (UK) Ltd, Croydon CR0 4YY
All rights reserved

Text © Francesca Simon, 2022
Illustrations © Steve May, 2022

The right of Francesca Simon and Steve May to be identified as author and
illustrator of this work respectively has been asserted in accordance with
Section 77 of the Copyright, Designs and Patents Act 1988

A CIP record for this book is available from the British Library

ISBN 978–0–571–34951–7

2 4 6 8 10 9 7 5 3 1

For Marta Fontanals-Simmons,
magic mezzo and the opera
queen of Niflheim.
F. S.

For Jackie, Andy and Yogi the dog
— my muse for Bitey-Bitey.
S. M.

Characters

Hack

Whack

Bitey-Bitey

Twisty Pants

Dirty Ulf

Elsa Gold-Hair

Contents

HACK GOES TO MARKET

Gaggala gaggala gu!

Gaggala gaggala gu!

Hack opened one eye.

Whack opened one eye.

GAGGALA GAGGALA GU!

Gaggala gaggala gu!
Gaggala gaggala gu!

Why were those stupid roosters crowing? How could it be time to get up? It was too dark and too cold. Mum hadn't even made up the hearth fire yet.

Whack pulled the shaggy fur cover over his head.

'I need my rest,' yawned Whack. 'My bones, my aching bones,' he moaned.

'Get up, you lazy lumps!' shouted Mum. She yanked the fur off their sleeping bench. 'It's market day.'

Hack sat up, shivering.

Whack sat up, shivering.

Hack and Whack loved and hated going to the Bear Island market.

They loved seeing all the

wonderful things there.

They hated that they were never allowed to bring any of them home.

Instead they had to trudge for ages through snow and rain and ice, laden with furs or cheese. Then, when they **finally** got to the market, they had to tag along while their mother traded the cheese for fishing hooks, or the furs for an ivory comb or an iron pan.

'I don't want to go,' said Hack. 'It's boring.'

'Me neither,' said Whack. 'I'm too tired.'

'You can go to the market or you can stay here and clean dirt and grease from the sheep's wool,' said Mum. 'And soak and scrape the sheepskins. **And** wash the clothes and sweep—'

'All right, I'll go,' said Hack.

'I'm staying,' said Whack. He huddled back under the fur cover.

He'd find some way of avoiding all those chores, even if he had to hide in the storeroom all day.

'I'm sending you on your own today, Hack,' said Mum. 'I'm too busy here. But you know what to do. You trade the cheeses for two soapstone bowls and some salt, if you can find some. Oh, and while you're at it, take Pecky-Pecky and see if you can trade her for some walrus meat.'

Plod all the way to the market carrying Pecky-Pecky, the world's meanest chicken?

'No way,' said Hack. 'She'll eat me alive before I'm halfway there. No one's ever going to buy that evil bird.'

Pecky-Pecky was too tough to eat, and too fierce to get eggs from. Even the family's wolf cub, Bitey-Bitey, was scared of her. Pecky-Pecky was one bad bird.

Mum sighed. 'All right,' she

BWAARK!

said. 'Heave your bones and go.
I've packed the cheeses for you.
And what's the golden rule?'

'If you can, RAID! If you can't,
TRADE!' yelled Hack.

Mum beamed. 'And no dawdling,' she added. 'Whack!' she shouted, poking the snoozing Viking. 'Get up before the trolls take you.'

'Nooooooooooooo,' groaned Whack.

Hack and Bitey-Bitey set off along the coastal sheep track towards the market, crunching through tufts of grassy moss flecked with frost. Icy mountains loomed across the water. All too soon, winter was coming.

Hack spotted Dirty Ulf and Twisty Pants walking ahead and ran to catch up, dodging around some wandering sheep. Twisty Pants was leading a skinny cow. Dirty Ulf was covered in even more soot and dirt than usual, and she smelled of burnt cloth.

'What happened to you?' said

Hack breathlessly.

'Fire Hazard has done it again,' said Dirty Ulf. 'He set fire to the smithy. Why he doesn't try to burn down the bathhouse I'll never know.'

Fire Hazard was Dirty Ulf's little brother. He was always smiling and laughing, but whenever he got his grubby hands on any kindling, watch out.

'What have you been sent to buy, Dirty Ulf?'

'A copper pot,' boasted Dirty Ulf.

'Wow,' said Hack. 'Really?' Hack stared at Dirty Ulf. She had no idea her family was so wealthy. Had her father been especially lucky in last summer's raids?

Dirty Ulf snorted. 'I was joking. Who can afford a copper cauldron? Mum wants cutting shears.'

'I'm getting a bucket,' said Twisty Pants.

'For a cow?' said Hack.

'Of course not,' said Twisty Pants. 'I have to sell her for two ounces of silver, buy a bucket and bring home the rest. Lucky you found me today because I'm a great trader. I once got a gold arm band in exchange for a silver penny.'

'How'd you do that?' said Dirty Ulf.

'Easy,' bragged Twisty Pants. 'I told him the penny was magic and granted three wishes, and he swapped.'

'Wait. You traded a magic coin for a gold arm band? You could have **wished** for a gold arm band and still had two wishes left,' said Dirty Ulf.

'Oh,' said Twisty Pants.

'What happened to the gold arm band?' said Hack.

'I buried it,' said Twisty Pants.

'And one day I'll remember where.'

The Viking band carried on trudging along the winding coastal path. Why did the market have to be so far away? Why did it have to be so cold?

Hack sighed.

Dirty Ulf yawned.

Twisty Pants sighed and yawned.

'Are we there yet?' moaned Twisty Pants.

'I'm hungry,' said Hack.

'Me too,' said Twisty Pants.

'Our mums wouldn't want us to **starve**, would they?' said Hack.

'No way,' said Twisty Pants.

They looked at the heavy knapsacks they were both carrying. Then they looked at each other.

'There's no harm in checking,' said Hack, reaching into her leather knapsack and unwrapping one of the pungent cheeses.

'It would be a shame to trade that cheese if it was bad,' said Twisty Pants.

'Rancid cheese? That would be terrible,' said Dirty Ulf. 'Your name would be soap. No one would ever trade with you again.'

'I'll taste a bit just to make sure,' said Hack, breaking off a fat chunk. 'Yup, it's good,' she said, chomping away.

'Hey, gimme some,' said Twisty Pants.

'And me, greedy guts,' said Dirty Ulf.

'You know I'm not allowed to share,' said Hack, taking another big bite.

Twisty Pants reached into his knapsack and removed a large hunk of warm bread. Twisty Pants's mum was famous for her grit-free bread.

Twisty Pants took a huge bite. 'Delicious,' he said.

'How about I trade you a hunk of bread for a hunk of cheese?' said Hack.

'Done,' said Twisty Pants, handing over a hunk of bread.

'That looks good,' said Dirty

Ulf. 'I forgot to bring any food with me. Mum tried to comb my hair and I ran away.'

Hack hesitated, then gave some cheese to Dirty Ulf. 'Terrible Vikings DON'T share. Don't tell **anyone** I shared this with you,' hissed Hack.

'I promise,' said Dirty Ulf.

Finally, they reached the headland. A merchant ship floated in the harbour below and the market bustled with stalls. Someone was roasting meat on a spit, which partially obscured the stink of the hides piled high. Stallholders shouted out, and traders bargained.

A great roar rang out as a huge man in a bearskin cloak pushed and shoved his way to the front of the roasting meat queue, bellowing curses and kicking aside anyone who stood in his way.

'Who's that man?' said Hack.

'Never seen him before,' said Twisty Pants.

'He's in a bad mood,' said Hack.

'Maybe he had a bath this morning,' said Dirty Ulf, shuddering.

'Look, he's raiding the meat stall!' said Hack, as the huge man yanked one of the joints off the spit and stomped towards the harbour, tearing at the dripping

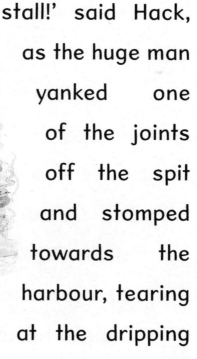

meat with his teeth while the crowds scattered.

Wow, thought Hack. No need to wonder whether the Bear-Man had raided or traded.

Hack, Dirty Ulf and Twisty Pants wandered amongst the market stalls. There was amber and furs and glass cups and axes and swords and bear hides  and jewellery and walrus tusks and hunting

falcons. Of course there were also boring things like  padlocks and loom weights and spoons and geese and pigs.

Twisty Pants went off to sell his cow. Bitey-Bitey stood hopefully in front of the roasting meat.

'Maybe they'll have honey cakes today,' said Dirty Ulf.

'Honey cakes,' said Hack.

Her mouth watered just thinking about them. Once, only once, there had been a market stall selling honey cakes studded with nuts and apples. She'd never tasted anything so wonderful in her life. It was like eating a cloud dripping with sweetness.

Then Hack saw the blacksmith's booth. 'Do you think we could get one of those swords?'

she said, staring longingly at the finely decorated silver hilts on display.

'Not in exchange for cheeses,' said Dirty Ulf. 'Oh, look.' She pointed. 'Toys!'

Hack and Dirty Ulf crowded around the bone carver's stall decorated with hanging antlers and walrus tusks, where toys and games were spread on top of a brown bearskin.

'Dice!' said Hack. 'I've been wanting some for ages.'

'Raid or trade?' whispered Dirty Ulf.

Hack looked at the ferocious Viking guarding the stall while the carver whittled away at some antlers. 'Trade,' she

whispered sadly. Hack whipped out a cheese. The carved dice were hers in exchange.

'Oh, look over here,' said Hack. 'A spinning top!'

'Raid or trade?' whispered Dirty Ulf.

The ferocious Viking fingered his axe and whistled.

'Trade,' said Hack sadly. She opened her knapsack. The spinning top was hers for two cheeses.

'Look at those ivory chess pieces,' said Dirty Ulf. She picked one up and felt its elaborately carved surface. 'Dad LOVES board games,' said Dirty Ulf. 'I know he'd much rather have these pieces than cutting shears.'

'Of course he would,' said

Hack. 'It would be a crime not to get them.'

'Raid or trade?' whispered Dirty Ulf.

The ferocious Viking stood in front of the chess pieces and folded his arms.

'Trade,' said Hack glumly.

Dirty Ulf handed over two broken pieces of silver coin and three amber beads. The bone carver weighed the silver on some scales and frowned.

Dirty Ulf handed over another broken piece of silver.

'It's all I've got,' said Dirty Ulf.

The bone carver weighed the silver and smiled.

And then Hack saw the cake stall.

'Look! Oh, look,' she breathed, heading over to the merchant tents. 'Honey cakes!'

'Honey cakes!' said Dirty Ulf, clutching her sack of chess pieces.

'Awhooo!' howled Bitey-Bitey.

Here was the magical stall Hack had dreamed about, piled high with honey cakes, like towers of deliciousness. The irresistible honeycomb smell wafted over them.

'Wow!' said Hack.

'Wow!' said Dirty Ulf.

'Raid or trade?' muttered Hack.

'Raid!' hissed Dirty Ulf.

'You distract him, and I'll grab the cakes,' whispered Hack.

The Vikings slowly crept up to the cake stall, one on either side. The stallholder was busy rearranging his wares with his back turned.

The Vikings reached out their hands—

'Stop right there,' shouted the baker, whipping round. 'Don't even **think** of stealing.'

Rats.

'We were just looking,' protested Hack.

'Who'd want your horrible cakes anyway?' said Dirty Ulf.

'Yeah,' said Twisty Pants, running up to join them.

'C'mon, everyone, we'll find better cakes somewhere else,' said Hack, stalking off.

The baker was so busy watching the young Vikings walk away he did not see a creeping wolf cub ...

Sneak ...

Sneak ...

Leap!

Bitey-Bitey jumped on the stall and snatched a dripping cake. Then he bolted, knocking over the stall and scattering cakes everywhere.

The three terrible Vikings grabbed as many cakes as they could, then ran for their lives until they were safely back on the headland.

Then they stopped and feasted.

'Yum!' said Hack. 'No more baked seaweed for us.'

'Of course **we** have cake every night,' bragged Twisty Pants.

'I could eat honey cake forever,' said Dirty Ulf, licking the last crumbs from her fingers.

'Wait till I tell you about **my** fantastic trade,' said Twisty Pants. 'A man with a long dark cloak came up to me and asked if I wanted to see something special. Then he opened his fist and he was holding five beans.

'"These aren't ordinary beans," the man said to me. "These are magic grow-ogre beans. Plant them and you can grow your very own pet ogres!

Someone offered me twenty-four sheep for just one of these beans. But because you look like such a fierce Viking, I'll let you have all five for that old cow."

'So we swapped,' boasted Twisty Pants. 'What a bargain. Five magic beans for one skinny old cow.'

'I'd love a pet ogre,' said Dirty Ulf. 'I could teach it to do tricks.'

'Wow. What a haul. We've got honey cakes and toys and chess pieces and grow-ogre beans,' said Hack. 'We are **great** Vikings.'

'Dad will be so pleased with those ivory chess pieces,' said

Dirty Ulf.

'And I can't wait to see Mum's face when I show her my magic beans,' said Twisty Pants.

'You ... traded ... the ... cow ... for ... some ... beans?' said Twisty Pants's mother slowly.

'**Magic** beans,' said Twisty Pants, beaming.

'You traded the cow for some beans?' repeated

Twisty Pants's mother.

'Yes! **Magic** beans,' said Twisty Pants, handing them to her. 'We can grow ogres now. Isn't that great?'

'You traded the cow for some beans?' yelled his mother.

For some reason his mum did not look like a mum who was about to organise feasts and sing songs in his honour.

'AAAARRRGGGGHHHH!'

she wailed, hurling the beans
out the door into the snow.
'AAAAAAARRRG
GGHH!' shrieked his mum
again.

Meanwhile back at Hack's longhouse ... Whack stirred the soup dolefully, tired after a long, hard day of chores.

'Hack, how did you get on at market today then? Did you raid or trade?' said Dad.

'Raid!' shouted Hack.

'Great job,' said Dad.

'That's my girl,' said Mum.

Whack scowled.

'Now where are my bowls and salt?' said Mum.

Hack looked at Mum.

Mum looked at Hack.

Hack had completely forgotten what she'd been sent to buy. 'No bowls and salt there today,' said Hack.

'So where's the cheese?' said Mum.

'Well,' said Hack. 'Er ... we were almost at the market when an enormous giant ambushed us, grabbed our knapsacks and stole all the cheeses. I tried to stop him but we had to run away or he would have eaten us too.'

'Hack, you are a **terrible** Viking!' said Whack, snatching the last honey cake before Hack could stop him.

HACK AND WHACK'S FIRST DAY AT VIKING SCHOOL

The Viking village was buzzing.

'Have you heard the news?' asked Olga Fish-Belly, dunking a filthy cloak in the icy stream.

'What?' said Hildi Horn-

Head, scrubbing some enormous underpants.

'Thorkel the Stout wants to start a school here,' said Olga.

Thorkel the Stout had recently moved to Bear Island – after a dispute with a fierce berserker warrior about who had the best beard – and it turned out Thorkel had lots of new-fangled ideas.

Grim Grit-Teeth gasped.

Hildi Horn-Head stopped scrubbing.

Glumra Bug-Bear dropped the petticoats she'd washed in the mud.

'Why would anyone want to start a **school**?' said Hack and Whack's mother.

'We teach children everything they need to know at home,' said Dirty Ulf's mother. 'Fire-making and ship-building and fence-mending ...'

'Thorkel wants to teach reading and writing runes. And counting,' said Olga Fish-Belly.

'**What?**' said Glumra.

'Ridiculous,' said Hildi.

'Though I heard that everyone on Bad Island is learning to write runes,' said Helga Gold-Hair.

'Oh?' said Olga.

'Oh?' said Glumra.

'Oh?' said Grim.

That was a whale of a different colour.

Bad Island was their sworn enemy. If those evil, no-good Vikings were learning to write, it could only be for one reason.

'They'll be sending us more curses on rune sticks,' said Olga Fish-Belly.

Bad Island was famous for their terrible curses. Everyone remembered the day a curse stick washed up on Bear Island's shore. No one could read the runes, but everyone was sure they knew what was written.

'I was told it said, **May you grow like a leek with your head in the ground**,' muttered Glumra Bug-Bear.

'It definitely said, **May flies enter your mouth every**

time you
open it,'
m u m b l e d
Grim Grit-Teeth.

'Nope! I know it said, **May you turn into a pancake and be eaten by trolls,'** said Dirty Ulf's mother.

55

'You're all wrong! It said,
**May a sea monster attack
your shore!**' shouted Hildi
Horn-Head.

'SHHHH! Not so loud, Hildi!'
yelped everyone.

'You have to be careful

repeating curses,' whispered Olga.

'Sorry,' said Hildi Horn-Head.

'Maybe we should give Thorkel's school a chance,' said Dirty Ulf's mum.

'Maybe we should,' said Hack and Whack's mum. 'What harm could it possibly do?'

It was early afternoon in the height of winter and already dark. Rain thudded on the turf roof. Mum had finished drying the herring, and fish scales glimmered on the beaten earth floor.

'NO, NO, NO, NO, **NO!**' screamed Dad. 'No sword-fighting in the house.'

'But I'm on the attack,' said Hack.

'NO, NO, NO, NO, **NO!**' screamed Mum. 'Don't bang axes on the table.'

Hack threw down her sword.

Whack threw down his axe.
Then Whack pinched Hack.

Hack ran after him and knocked over the loom. She tripped and got tangled in the wool she'd been untangling.

Riiiip!

Mum's blanket.

She'd been weaving it for days
and days and days.

'Aarrrgggghh!' yelled Mum.

'Stand back! We're on the
attack!' shouted Whack.

'Hack and Whack, just stop!'
screamed Mum and Dad.

'What are we going to do?'
said Dad.

'They're the worst Vikings in
the village,' said Mum.

Hack cheered and whooped.

Whack cheered and yelped.

They loved being the best at something. Especially if it was the best at being worst.

Dad closed his eyes. For a brief moment, he thought about Elsa Gold-Hair. Of course he would **never** want **his** children to be goody-goodies like her. No way. How dreadful. How awful. A Viking who liked sharing would definitely come to a bad end.

But still, it would **occasionally** be nice to get a bit of peace and

quiet at home. If
only Hack and Whack
could be the worst Vikings
outside the longhouse.

'Hack and Whack need to learn discipline,' said Mum.

'No we don't,' said Hack, bouncing around and pretending she was a hungry bear waking from hibernation.

'No we don't,' said Whack, hopping up and down and pretending he was a wolf, hungry for some tasty bear.

'They can't run wild forever,' said Dad.

'Yes we can,' said Hack.

'They **could** go to school,' said Mum.

'School?' said Dad.

Hack stopped pretending she was a hungry bear.

Whack stopped pretending he was a prowling wolf.

'School?' said Hack.

'School?' said Whack.

'School,' said Mum. 'Thorkel the Stout is starting Bear Island's first school.'

Dad looked puzzled. 'Vikings don't need to go to school,' he said. 'We teach children everything they have to know.'

'They could learn to read and write runes,' said Mum.

Dad looked shocked. 'Read and write?' he said. 'No one

needs to learn to read and write.'

'And count,' said Mum.

'Vikings don't need to count,' said Dad. 'They're not going to school and that's fi—'

'It's winter,' said Mum. 'It would get Hack and Whack out of the longhouse for a few hours.'

'They'll start school tomorrow,' said Dad.

What?

'No way!' yelled Hack and Whack, running out the door into the rain.

They didn't stop running till they reached the harbour at the bottom of the village. The sea-

salt air stung their faces as they kicked the black sand. The ebb and flow of waves rustled the pebbles on the shore.

'What's school?' said Hack, stamping her feet to keep warm

and blowing on her chapped hands.

'I don't know,' said Whack.

Was school a far-off island they'd never heard of?

Was school a place you were sent when you were banished?

Was school the land of ogres and giants and trolls?

Whatever it was they did **NOT** want to go there.

'Vikings don't go to school,' said Hack. 'Dad said so.'

'Yeah,' said Whack.

'We're not going and that's that,' said Hack and Whack.

The next morning Dad marched Hack and Whack through the snowdrifts to school.

Hack kicked.

Whack screamed.

'WE DON'T WANT TO GO TO SCHOOL!' they shrieked.

'Too bad,' said Dad, pushing them through the door.

The schoolhouse was full of screaming children, jumping up and down on the benches and swinging their swords and axes.

'I don't want to be in school,' yelled Spear Nose.

'I don't want to be in school,' yelled Dirty Ulf.

'I don't want to be in school,' yelled Twisty Pants.

'I don't want to be in school,' yelled Stubbed Toe.

'I do,' said Elsa Gold-Hair.

A short man with a beard stood in front of the benches and tried to make himself heard above the uproar.

'Be quiet, children! Welcome to my brand-new Viking school.

I'm your teacher, Thorkel the Stout.'

Thorkel had looked forward to saying those words for months. He was far away from the fierce berserker he'd had that silly quarrel with. He'd started a school. And now all the children in the village would learn to read and write. He could already feel a poem coming ...

Now that we're all in school

Please, please don't play the fool.

There's no place here for hool-

igans ...

Yes, the poem needed work, but all in good time.

The shouting and screaming and kicking and hitting and yelling continued.

'Here in Viking school you will learn to read, write and count,' Thorkel roared.

Read? Write? Count?

'We want to learn how to build boats,' yelled Little Sparrow.

'We want to learn how to trick trolls and jinx giants,' shouted Loud Mouth.

'We want to learn how to fight,' screamed Scar Leg.

'We want to learn how to make axes,' roared Spear Nose.

'BE QUIET,' bellowed Thorkel. 'Now who's sitting up straight and ready to listen?'

Elsa Gold-Hair sat up straight.

Whack pulled Hack's pigtails.

Hack whacked Whack's helmet.

Spear Nose pushed them both off the bench.

Twisty Pants scratched his bottom.

No more Mr Nice Guy, thought Thorkel.

'Hooligans! How will you know how many swords and silver bracelets you've stolen if you can't count? How will you know who's grabbed the most gold if you can't count?'

Thorkel held up one finger. 'Now repeat after me: ONE ogre.'

Thorkel held up two fingers, adding more as he counted.

'TWO giants.

'THREE spears.

'FOUR goblins.

'FIVE axes.

'SIX dwarves.

'SEVEN trolls.

'EIGHT whales.

'NINE longboats ...'

No one except Elsa Gold-Hair paid any attention.

The shouting and screaming and kicking and hitting continued.

Maybe there is a reason that no one has ever set up a school on Bear Island before, thought Thorkel the Stout, watching the young Vikings running riot around the fire.

He tried again.

'And now it's time to learn to read and write runes. Isn't that exciting? Take out your knives and Elsa Gold-Hair will hand everyone a stick to carve on. We'll start with the rune called

feoh, the most important rune. It means wealth. And **ur**, for strength. Then there's **rad**—'

Thorkel droned on and on and on.

'Are we done yet?' yelled Loud Mouth, racing around the room.

'On your guard!' yelled Hack, whacking Whack with her rune stick.

'On **your** guard!' yelled Whack, whacking her back.

And then everyone started whacking and smacking.

Thorkel tried one last time.

'Class! Let's forget about

runes for today and learn some
terrible curses instead.'

Curses?

Hack and Whack stopped
smacking.

Loud Mouth and Spear Nose stopped whacking.

Stubbed Toe and Scar Leg stopped shrieking.

Twisty Pants stopped scratching.

Dirty Ulf sat up straight.

Curses? Terrible curses?

The Viking class fell silent. Finally, **finally**, they were learning something good.

Ah, thought Thorkel. **That's more like it.**

'Class, repeat after me: may you turn into a chicken and moo like a cow,' intoned Thorkel.

'May you turn into a chicken and moo like a cow,' chanted the young Vikings.

'May you grow donkey ears.'

'May you grow donkey ears.'

'May your
nose turn into
a turnip.'

**'May your
nose turn into a turnip.'**

'May your bottom always itch!'

**'May your bottom always
itch!'**

Over and over and louder and louder the Vikings chanted their hexes.

'Louder!' shouted Thorkel. 'Louder!' Finally, he was making progress. Tonight he'd start writing **The Saga of Thorkel the Stout** so everyone could learn about his great deeds.

'May you turn into a chicken and moo like a cow!' shrieked the class.

'May you grow donkey ears!'

'May your nose turn into a turnip!'

'May your bottom always itch!'

'MAY YOU—'

'RAAAAAA AAAAAAAA!'

A hideous, horrible roar shook the schoolhouse. Something

monstrous was stomping and howling outside.

The Viking class stopped cursing. Thorkel the Stout froze.

Had their curse worked? Was a giant mooing chicken with donkey ears, a turnip nose and an itchy bottom coming to attack them?

'RAAAAAAAAAA AAAA!' roared the creature. **'Where are you, Thorkel?'** it bellowed, pounding on the door until it splintered. **'Just wait till I get my hands on you, you maggot-mouthed son of a mare!'**

A furious face in a bearskin cloak smashed its way through the shattered door.

'Yikes,' said Hack.

'It's the Bear-Man from the market,' hissed Dirty Ulf.

'AAARRRRRGG GGHH!' shrieked Thorkel.

'Carry on cursing, class,' he managed to shout before turning and running out the back door.

The Bear-Man broke down the door and burst into the room. He shattered a bench, kicked over the table, and ran bellowing after Thorkel.

The class dashed to the door and saw Thorkel racing into the woods, chased by the roaring Bear-Man. Pecky-Pecky ran after them both.

'Does this mean no more school?' said Elsa Gold-Hair.

'I guess so,' said Hack.

'Shame,' said Dirty Ulf.

'I was starting to enjoy school,' said Whack, yawning.

'Me too,' said Twisty Pants.

'Sure beats gutting fish,' said Hack.

'And scraping sheepskins,' said Whack.

'I wonder if Thorkel will ever come back,' said Spear Nose.

'You maggot-mouthed son of a mare!' shrieked Hack, slashing at Whack with her sword.

'You stinky seal guts!' shrieked Whack, slashing at Hack with his axe.

Hack kicked over a bench.

Whack knocked over the table. Plates and knives and tankards crashed to the ground. The terrible twins jumped over the table and ran around it, hacking and whacking and screaming.

'Stop!' shouted Mum, carrying a plateful of herrings. 'What are you doing?'

'Playing Bear-Man Attacks,' said Hack, waving her sword.

'Thorkel the Stout ran away from school today,' said Whack, panting. 'He was chased by a huge man wearing a bearskin and stomping and roaring and swinging a club.'

'Put that table back the way you found it before your father gets home,' said Mum. 'You're the worst Vikings in the village. Bear-Men are called berserkers. They're horrible bullies and troublemakers.'

'So you've heard the bad news,' said Dad, walking into the longhouse and throwing down his fishing nets.

'What?' said Mum.

'The berserker Grunt Iron-Skull has moved in next door.'

Mum dropped the plate of herrings. 'Are you sure?' she whispered. 'Grunt Iron-Skull? He's moved in **next door**?'

'Yes, the world's worst neighbour, Grunt Iron-Skull, is

back from the wars,' said Dad.
He looked grim. 'He just picked
a fight with Bragi Bread-Nose.
And Thorkel the Stout barely
escaped with his life today.'

'I thought Grunt was dead,'
wailed Mum.

'If only,' said Dad. 'The world's
most terrible berserker is alive,
and—'

'He's living next door!' said
Hack and Whack.

Mum hid her face in her hands.

'We're doomed,' she said.

HACK AND WHACK AND GRUNT THE BERSERKER

Uggghhh.

What was that awful, stinky, whiffy, smelly pong filling their longhouse?

'It smells like a zillion ogres

have done a poo,' said Hack, coughing and choking.

'Oh gods, what a stink,' gasped Dad, flinging his cloak over his head.

'Bitey-Bitey, was that you?' said Mum, waving her hands in front of her face.

Bitey-Bitey slunk off and hid behind the loom.

'Are the cows sick?' asked Dad.

'They seemed fine when I

cleaned out the cowshed,' said Mum.

She opened the door and popped her head out. Then she quickly stepped back inside and slammed the door.

'Grunt Iron-Skull has built a

privy against our back wall,' she gasped, sinking down on the bench. 'How dare he!'

Grunt Iron-Skull was the fiercest, scariest Viking in the world. His bellow could blow down a house. He foamed at the mouth. He bit holes in his shield.

Ogres heard him stomping and ran away.

Giants burst into tears.

Trolls hid.

The undead decided they'd
rather be dead.

No one messed with Grunt
Iron-Skull. Or his hel-hound,
Muddy Butt — the fiercest,
nastiest dog that ever walked
the earth.

And now Grunt had built a

privy right against Hack and Whack's longhouse.

'He should build his toilet next to his own house, like everyone else,' said Hack.

'Yeah,' said Whack.

'And who's going to make him?' said Mum.

'Not me,' said Dad. 'He'd tear my head off.'

'Not me,' said Mum. 'He'd eat my ears.'

Hack looked at Whack.

Whack looked at Hack.
They'd never seen
Mum and Dad look so
scared.

A terrible rumbling,
grumbling explosion
erupted, followed by the
worst smell Hack and
Whack had ever smelled.
Worse than rotting whale
carcasses.

Worse than rotting seals. Worse than the worst stink in the world multiplied by a million billion stinks.

'Oh no. He's doing **another** poo!' wailed Whack.

'What are we going to do?' said Dad.

'Let's ask the chieftain for help,' said Mum.

They found Thrain Scatter-Brain on his turf roof trying to shoo some goats off it.

'We need you to tell Grunt Iron-Skull to move his privy away from our wall,' said Dad.

Thrain Scatter-Brain went pale.

'Shark's teeth,' gasped Thrain Scatter-Brain. 'He'd go berserk. He'd scrunch me into a ball and kick me into the next valley.'

'But you're the chieftain. Who else will tell him if you don't?' said Mum.

Thrain Scatter-Brain shrugged. 'Grunt Iron-Skull is **your**

neighbour. You deal with it. Now
shoo, **shoo**, you silly goat!'

Mum, Dad, Hack and Whack

trudged back to their longhouse. Not even their smoking fire and the fishy smell from their oil lamps could cover up the horrible stench coming from Grunt's privy.

'I think I'm going to move into the cowshed,' said Dad.

'I'll join you,' said Mum.

'I can't stand this stink a minute longer,' wailed Hack.

'The smell will kill me,' wailed Whack.

'Who will rid us of this hideous fiend?' said Dad.

Hack picked up her sword.

Whack picked up his axe.

'We're Hack and Whack, on the attack!' yelled Whack. **'We'll** tell him to move his privy.'

Hack and Whack charged out the door and stomped down the muddy path leading to Grunt Iron-Skull's massive, nail-studded front door. Bitey-Bitey crept after them, whimpering.

'We'll chase that berserker off,' said Hack.

'Yeah,' said Whack. 'We'll make him sorry he ever came back from the wars.'

Knock.

Knock.

Knock.

A horrible howling burst from inside Grunt's decrepit longhouse, as if the fiends of hel had just been unleashed and were looking for a snack. And not a healthy one.

Stomp!

Stomp!

Stomp!

The door was flung open. The giant berserker filled the entire doorway. He held a gigantic axe in one of his gigantic fists.

His hideous hound Muddy Butt
snarled and slathered behind
him.

Grunt Iron-Skull looked down at the two terrible Vikings. 'What do you want?' he growled.

Hack gulped.

'Spit it out!' roared Grunt.

'Grunt Iron-Skull. We demand you move your privy away from our longhouse immediately,' squeaked Hack.

'Yeah,' piped Whack. 'Or else.'

Bitey-Bitey snarled.

Grunt's hel-hound Muddy Butt roared. Muddy Butt looked

like he gobbled walruses for breakfast, bears for lunch, and little Vikings and wolf cubs for an afternoon snack.

Bitey-Bitey ran away as fast as his paws would carry him.

'If you aren't gone by the time I count to ...' Grunt Iron-Skull paused. He couldn't count higher than one. He usually snarled 'Gimme!' when he wanted something and that normally worked out just fine.

'If you aren't gone by the time I count to one,' roared Grunt Iron-Skull, 'I'll bang you flat as pancakes.'

Hack and Whack did not want to be banged flat as pancakes. They ran off and hid in the storehouse behind a barrel of ale. Behind them they heard Grunt's door slam shut.

Hack turned and stuck out her tongue.

'Ya boo sucks, you heap of

whale blubber,' shrieked Hack.

'You big meanie,' shrieked Whack.

'Son of a mare!'

'Pig's bladder!'

'Stinky troll!'

'Walrus breath!'

'Seal flipper!'

'Maggot mouth!'

'Troll belly button!' bellowed Hack.

Hack and Whack sat
by the loom inside
their longhouse, slowly
cleaning the greasy,
freshly shorn wool. Both
had cloths wrapped
tightly round their noses
and mouths. But not
even the reek of cow
urine or the sweet-
smelling cauldron of

simmering soup suspended over the fire could block the stench coming from Grunt's privy.

'I can't stand this!' shrieked Hack.

'I'm going to die if I sit here being poisoned a second longer!' shrieked Whack.

Mum came in from the bathhouse, drying her hair. She coughed and choked as she entered.

'I want you two to go and

gather puffin eggs on the cliffs,' said Mum.

For the first time in their lives, Hack and Whack did not wait to be asked twice.

Hack grabbed her sword.

Whack grabbed his axe.

'And remember, collect as many eggs as you can,' said Mum. **'NO SHARING!'**

'No sharing,' agreed Hack and Whack. As if they would ever do anything so dreadful.

They snatched up two baskets
and ran outside into the spring
sunshine and the salty fresh air.
Trickles of heat were already
warming the frozen land. The

sun months would soon be here.

They found Twisty Pants and Dirty Ulf gathering seabird eggs on the jutting black cliffs. Gulls screeched and whirled and flapped around them, calling **Kreeea! Kreeea! Kreeea!** as the Vikings shook their cloaks to scare them off.

'What are we going to do about Grunt?' wailed Hack, pushing Whack aside to snatch an egg.

'We'll have to run away to Greenland,' said Whack, shoving her back and grabbing the rest of the eggs from the nest. 'Anything to get away from his privy.'

'We're Hack and Whack, not on the attack ...' moaned Hack and Whack. They sat down on the mossy cliffs and watched the waves crash against the rocks while the wind blew spray onto their faces.

Twisty Pants and Dirty Ulf

joined them.

'Grunt the berserker has built a privy against our longhouse and everyone is too scared to do anything about it,' said Hack.

'Lucky I'm here,' said Twisty Pants, trying and failing to straighten his leggings. 'I've fought loads of berserkers,' he bragged.

'What makes them go berserk?' asked Dirty Ulf.

'They go berserk when they
smell ... burnt porridge,' said
Twisty Pants. 'So when I fought
one, I sneaked up behind
him, yelled "BOO!" and held

a cauldron of burnt porridge under his nose and he ran off shrieking and was never seen again.'

'**You** saw Grunt when he burst into the school,' said Hack. 'Berserkers are as strong as bears, nothing scares them, and Dad says neither fire nor iron can harm them.'

'Yikes,' said Dirty Ulf.

'I knew that,' said Twisty Pants.

'And we've got one living next door!' wailed Whack.

'When are you going to fight him then, Twisty Pants?' said Dirty Ulf.

'Right away,' said Twisty Pants. He stood up. Then he scratched his head. 'But I think it would be better to send him something to scare him first.'

'A bathtub,' said Dirty Ulf.

'Even scarier,' said Hack.

'A skull covered in curses,'

said Whack.

'I'm not sure there are any spare skulls lying around,' said Hack.

'Or we could write some on a rune stick,' said Dirty Ulf.

Hack looked at Whack.

Wow. Why hadn't they thought of that?'

'That is a brilliant idea, Dirty Ulf,' said Hack. 'We can leave a message outside his door, like, **Beware, smelly pants,** or,

Get out of here, you big meanie.'

'Yeah,' said Twisty Pants.

'There's just one problem,' said Hack. 'Who knows how to write runes?'

'Not me,' said Whack. He hadn't paid any attention on the one day he went to school.

'Me neither,' said Hack.

'Leave it to me,' said Twisty Pants. 'I'll write such a scary message that Grunt will run away forever when he sees it. But you'll need to fill my basket with eggs in payment.'

Hand over some eggs? Hack and Whack would pay a lot more to get rid of Grunt and his privy. They emptied their eggs into Twisty Pants's basket.

Twisty Pants took out his knife and started carving runes on a fat stick.

Elsa Gold-Hair wandered over, her blue cloak flapping in

the wind. Naturally her baskets
had three times more eggs than
anyone else's.

'What are you doing?' said
Elsa. She sat down on her
cloak, and carefully placed her
baskets in front of her.

'We're getting ready to fight a berserker,' said Dirty Ulf.

'There!' said Twisty Pants proudly, brandishing the rune stick. The young Vikings gathered round to admire it.

'What does it say?' asked Hack.

'It says, **Move this privy, you wobbly lump of walrus blubber, or a witch will bite your bum**.'

'That's perfect,' said Hack.

This was sure to do the trick. Their misery would soon be over.

'Hang on. Let me see,' said Elsa.

Elsa grabbed Twisty Pants's rune stick.

'This is just gobbledygook,' said Elsa Gold-Hair. 'It says, **torch serpent fire mother fish . . . squiggle, squiggle, squiggle**.'

'You said you could write, Twisty Pants!' said Hack.

'I **can** write,' said Twisty Pants. 'I didn't say I **knew** what I was writing.'

'Give us our eggs back,' shouted Hack and Whack.

'No way!' said Twisty Pants, holding tight to his basket.

Hack grabbed the basket.

Whack grabbed the basket.

Smash! Crash!

All the eggs rolled out and over the cliffs, cracking on the rocks below.

'Oops,' said Hack.

Hack, Whack, Dirty Ulf and Twisty Pants looked at Elsa's overflowing egg baskets.

'What?' said Elsa Gold-Hair.

'Elsa, you know we're not allowed to share,' said Hack.

'We'd get into big trouble if we did,' said Whack.

'But **you** are,' said Hack.

'So you should share your eggs with us,' said Whack.

'Sharing means what's yours is ours and what's mine is mine,' said Hack.

Elsa sighed. There was **something** wrong with what Hack and Whack were saying, but she couldn't quite put her finger on it. 'Okay, I'll share my eggs with you,' she said.

The young Vikings were so busy grabbing Elsa's eggs that they didn't notice Bitey-Bitey creeping closer and closer to the rune stick.

Bitey-Bitey loved sticks. Especially lovely fat ones. His humans burnt wood and never left any twigs for him.

SNATCH!

Bitey-Bitey nabbed the rune stick and ran off.

Bitey-Bitey raced back to the longhouse holding his prize. He knew the perfect spot to bury his treasure. Quickly, the wolf cub started digging next to Grunt's stinky outhouse.

A shadow fell across him. Bitey-Bitey looked up and saw

Muddy Butt looming above him.

'GGRRRRRRRRR!'

snarled Muddy Butt.

Bitey-Bitey dropped the stick and ran.

Grunt Iron-Skull stared at the carvings on the rune stick. What were these foul curses Muddy Butt had brought into his home? Of course Grunt couldn't read, but he knew curses when he saw them.

Some fiendish enemy was cursing him. But who? Who? What living person would dare threaten Grunt Iron-Skull?

Or could it be an evil ghoul or ghost? Grunt shuddered.

Uggghhh. A ghost had once sat down next to him at a feast and drunk all his mead. Another had crept into his storehouse and snatched all his dried fish.

Grunt hurled the stick into the

fire. Bah! Ghost or not, it would take more than a few hexes to scare **him.**

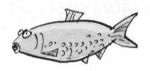

The smell was worse than ever.

'**How** can we get Grunt to leave?' wailed Whack.

'We **have** to scare him away,' said Dirty Ulf.

'But **how**?' said Hack. 'He's bigger and meaner and

stronger than anyone in the village.'

'What's the scariest thing you know?' said Twisty Pants.

'Baths,' said Dirty Ulf, shuddering.

'Whale blubber,' said Whack.

'Of course, **nothing** scares me,' bragged Twisty Pants.

Elsa Gold-Hair considered. 'Ghosts!'

Everyone was scared of ghosts. And ghouls. And things

that go bump in the night.

'Elsa, you are a genius,' said
Hack.

It was past evening meal, in the
deepest darkest dead of night.
Mum, Dad, Hack and Whack sat
up by the hearth fire, waiting.
Mum wove at the loom, Dad
mended fishing nets by the

smoky fish-oil lamp. Hack and Whack played board games.

Finally there was the familiar sound of stomping footsteps, and someone entering Grunt's privy.

'Start now,' whispered Mum.

'Dad!' said Hack loudly. 'What did you say about the headless ghoul? He's back?'

'Yes,' replied Dad loudly. 'I saw Thord the Evil last night, right outside Grunt Iron-Skull's privy.'

'Was he carrying his head?' said Whack.

'Yes!' said Mum. 'You know he was killed on that very spot.'

'Everyone keep away from that privy!' shouted Dad. 'Thord the Evil is lonely! He'll pull you down into his tomb and block the entrance forever.'

'And if the moonlight flashes on his rolling eyeballs you'll be trapped with him in that stinking bog,' said Mum.

'Thord the Evil won't stop haunting us until that privy is sealed up,' yelled Dad.

'It's amazing Grunt is still alive,' yelled Hack.

'Not for long!' said Mum.

'You wouldn't catch me sitting on that toilet seat,' shouted Dad. 'Not if you gave me a hundred ox hides.'

'I'm glad I'm not Grunt Iron-Skull,' shouted Mum.

Grunt heard everything through
the thin privy wall. He shuddered.
A headless ghoul was living

beneath his toilet? Did that mean that at any moment—

Wait.

Was something creeping outside? Was Thord the Evil coming for him?

Or ... horrors! Was Thord **already** inside the privy?

Suddenly something banged hard on the wall.

And then there was a high-pitched shriek.

'AAAARRGGGGHHHH!'

yelped Grunt.

He jumped off the loo as fast as he could, kicked aside the flimsy privy walls, rolled an enormous boulder over the hole — and ran for his life.

Hack and Whack woke the next morning to the warm, familiar

smells of peat, smoke, sheep's wool, cows and wet thatch.

Then Hack sniffed again.

Whack sniffed again.

Something was missing.

'Where's the stink?' said Hack.

They crept outside. Grunt's privy had gone. A huge stone covered the pit hole.

Could it be? Had the miracle happened?

Dirty Ulf, Twisty Pants and Elsa Gold-Hair saw them and ran over.

'Did you hear us stomping last night?' said Dirty Ulf.

'We did!' said Hack.

'And I whacked the wall,' boasted Twisty Pants.

'And I screamed,' said Elsa Gold-Hair.

'It sounded like you were being eaten by a shapeshifter,' said Whack.

'It turns out I am good at screaming,' said Elsa Gold-Hair.

Mum and Dad appeared from the storeroom.

'Have you heard the news?' said Mum. 'Grunt Iron-Skull and Muddy Butt have gone off to

fight in King Olaf's army.'

'HURRAH!' cheered Hack and Whack.

'We'll be feasting tonight,' said Dad. 'And you are all invited.'

THE END

ACKNOWLEDGEMENTS

Many thanks to Isla Steyn and Joshua Stamp-Simon, for their help in creating the ferocious chicken, Pecky-Pecky.

TWO TERRIBLE VIKINGS

International bestselling author of **HORRID HENRY**

FRANCESCA SIMON

Illustrated by Steve May

Have you read
Hack and Whack's
first adventures?

Set in the snowy fjords of a Viking kingdom, the terrible twins, Hack and Whack, are proud to be the best worst vikings. Nothing stops the marauding pair as they steal boats, loot a birthday party, track a troll and sail off to raid Bad Island with their friends Twisty Pants and Dirty Ulf.

Well, almost nothing . . .